Dial Books for Young Readers, an imprint of Penguin Random House, LLC, New York

Copyright © 2019 by Jon Agee

Visit us online at penguinrandomhouse.com • Printed in China • ISBN 9780525555469 • Design by Lily Malcom • Text set in Clarendon Text Pro

10 9 8 7 6 5 4 3 2 1

Jon Agee

I WANT A DOG

Welcome to Happydale Animal Shelter.
Are you looking for a porcupine?
A weasel?
I've got an adorable armadillo.

No, thank you.
I want a dog.

A dog is an excellent choice.
A dog makes an excellent pet.

But wouldn't you prefer this awesome anteater?

No.

How about this baby baboon? It doesn't go woof, but it chases a ball, just like a dog!

I don't want a baby baboon.

How about this python? It doesn't have legs,
but it slithers over when you call it.

I don't want a python.

How about this frog? It can hide a bone,
and it barks at passing cars, just like a dog.

That's not true.
Frogs don't bark
or hide bones.
And besides,
I want a dog.

Look what I found! A goldfish! It wags its tail, and knows how to play dead, just like a dog.

**Mister, that goldfish
is not *playing* dead.**

I'm sorry, I didn't mean to bring you a dead goldfish.

That's okay.
I don't want a goldfish.
I want a dog.

Very well! Wait right here. I'll get the dog.

Here is the dog!

Mister, this is not a dog.
This is a lizard *dressed
up* as a dog.

Yes, you're right,
but you could train it to go *woof*.

I don't want to train
a lizard to go *woof!*
I want a *dog* that
goes *woof!*

Would you consider this albatross? This kangaroo? This darling wombat?

No!
No!
And no!

Excuse me,
mister. I have one
simple question:
Do you even
have a dog?

No, I don't.

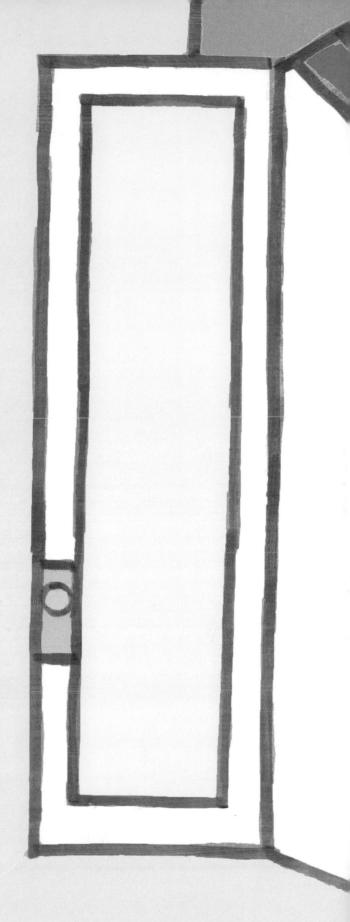

**Well then,
I'm leaving
right now!**

Wait!

Before you go, would you please tell me what's so special about a dog?

Sure!

A dog is
loyal,
loving,
smart,
cuddly,
goofy,
courageous . . .
and it's the best friend
you could ever have in the world.

Actually, I might have the perfect pet. It's not a dog, but it sounds exactly like what you described.

No! Stop!
PLEASE,
don't bother!

This is Lucinda!
She eats twenty pounds of
fish every day and needs
to swim in at least 3,000
cubic feet of salt water.

I'll take her!

Wow.

Who ever heard of an animal shelter
that doesn't have a dog?

But that's okay.
Dogs are overrated.